THE MOON SHINES DOWN

Text © 2008 by Roberta Rauch (estate of Margaret Wise Brown).
Illustrations © 2008 by Linda Bleck.

Published in Nashville, Tennessee, by Thomas Nelson. Thomas Nelson is a
registered trademark of Thomas Nelson, Inc.

Thomas Nelson, Inc., titles may be purchased in bulk for educational, business,
fund-raising, or sales promotional use. For information, please e-mail
SpecialMarkets@ThomasNelson.com.

ISBN 978-1-4003-1299-3 (hardcover w/jacket)
ISBN 978-1-4003-1401-0 (scholastic edition)

Library of Congress Cataloging-in-Publication Data
Brown, Margaret Wise, 1910–1952.
  The moon shines down / Margaret Wise Brown and Laura Minchew.
      p. cm.
  Illustrated by Linda Bleck.
  ISBN 978-1-4003-1299-3 (hardback)
  1. Prayers—Juvenile literature. I. Minchew, Laura. II. Bleck, Linda. III. Title.
BV265.B69 2008
242'.62—dc22
                      2008023070

Printed in China
08 09 10 11 12 MT 5 4 3 2 1

THE MOON SHINES DOWN

Margaret Wise Brown

with additional verses by
Laura Minchew

Illustrated by
Linda Bleck

THOMAS NELSON
Since 1798

NASHVILLE   DALLAS   MEXICO CITY   RIO DE JANEIRO   BEIJING

The Story Behind the Lost Manuscript . . .

The Moon Shines Down
from MARGARET WISE BROWN,
the Author of *Goodnight Moon*

The Moon Shines Down is being published for the first time fifty-six years after the death of the beloved children's author Margaret Wise Brown.

Amazingly, this unpublished manuscript lay forgotten in a cedar trunk in a Vermont barn. When it was discovered, the onionskin paper had yellowed and the paperclips that held the pages together had rusted.

Based on the New England sampler prayer, "God Bless the Moon and God Bless Me," this soon-to-be bedtime classic is a prayer for God's blessing on all the world's children.

However, the manuscript was incomplete, too short for a standard size picture book. Children's book publisher, Laura Minchew, a longtime fan of Brown, took on the challenge to complete the work. Laura was able to match Margaret Wise Brown's writing style, capturing Brown's unique rhythms and rhyme schemes.

The wonderful result you hold in your hands introduces a timeless Margaret Wise Brown book to delight a new generation of children the world over.

The Moon shines down and sheds its beams
On a house with a stork where a Dutch boy dreams
Of tulip fields by quiet streams
In his flat Dutch Land of cheese and creams.

I see the Moon and the Moon sees me,
And the Moon sees the Dutch boy
Far over the sea.
When the tulips bloom by the Zuider Zee,
O God bless him and God bless me.

In Switzerland
Where the cowbells ring,
The Moon shines down
And the Nightingales sing.
The mountains rise
Into moonlit skies,
And the children dream of edelweiss.

I see the Moon and the Moon sees me
That shone last night on the Swiss Country.
O God bless the Moon
And God bless me,
And the children asleep
In the Swiss Country.

Across the sea in the Far, Far East,
The sun comes up as we go to sleep.
Many languages these children speak—
Japanese, Korean, and Chinese,
Mandarin, Laotian, and Vietnamese.

God bless the Moon
And God bless me,
And God bless the children
In the Far, Far East.

The Moon shines down on Mexico
Where Iguanas creep
Steady and slow,
The Toucan sleeps in her nest,
And children lay their heads to rest,
Thanking God that they are blessed.

I see the Moon
And the Moon sees me,
And the Moon sees the kids in Mexico.
God bless the Moon
And God bless me,
And God bless the Toucan with her funny nose.

Then the Moon shines down
On the Fields of France,
Where the little French children
Are jumping in a dance—
Hop, skip, jump, and one, two, three.
Little French children—oui, oui, oui, oui!

I see the Moon
And the Moon sees me,
And the little French children
Far over the sea.
God bless the Moon
And God bless me,
And the little French children—oui, oui, oui, oui!

The Moon shines down on the Outback Wild.
Too much to see for this sleepy child,
With a Joey snuggled in a Kangaroo pouch
And a Wallaby in the brambles . . . ouch!

God bless the Moon
And God bless me.
God bless the Koala in the eucalyptus tree,
And the Platypus,
And the tall Emu,
And the Australian kids with their backyard zoo.

When the moonlight shines
  On an English Wood,
    Where two little boys sleep as they should—
    Sound asleep while the Crickets peep
    And the Fireflies flicker beyond their sleep.

I see the Moon and the Moon sees me,
And the English boys sleeping close to the sea.
God bless the Moon
And God bless me,
And the English boys sleeping
Close to the sea.

In Africa where the Lion roars,
The Elephant stomps,
The Warthog snores,
The Moon shines down,
The warm breeze blows
And tickles the sleeping one's little nose.

I see the Moon and the Moon sees me,
And the Moon sees the children
In Zimbabwe
And all over Africa,
In fields and plains,
Children dance in summer rains.

The Moon shines bright
On this Christmas night.
A Caroler sings
By candlelight.
In my neighborhood,
The children dream
Of puppies, peppermints, and pretty things,
On this Holy Night
When all is right.

I see the Moon
And the Moon sees me,
And the Moon sees the Christ Child,
Heaven's Baby.
God bless the Moon
And God bless me,
(And God bless Christmas!)
And God bless the children
In my own country.

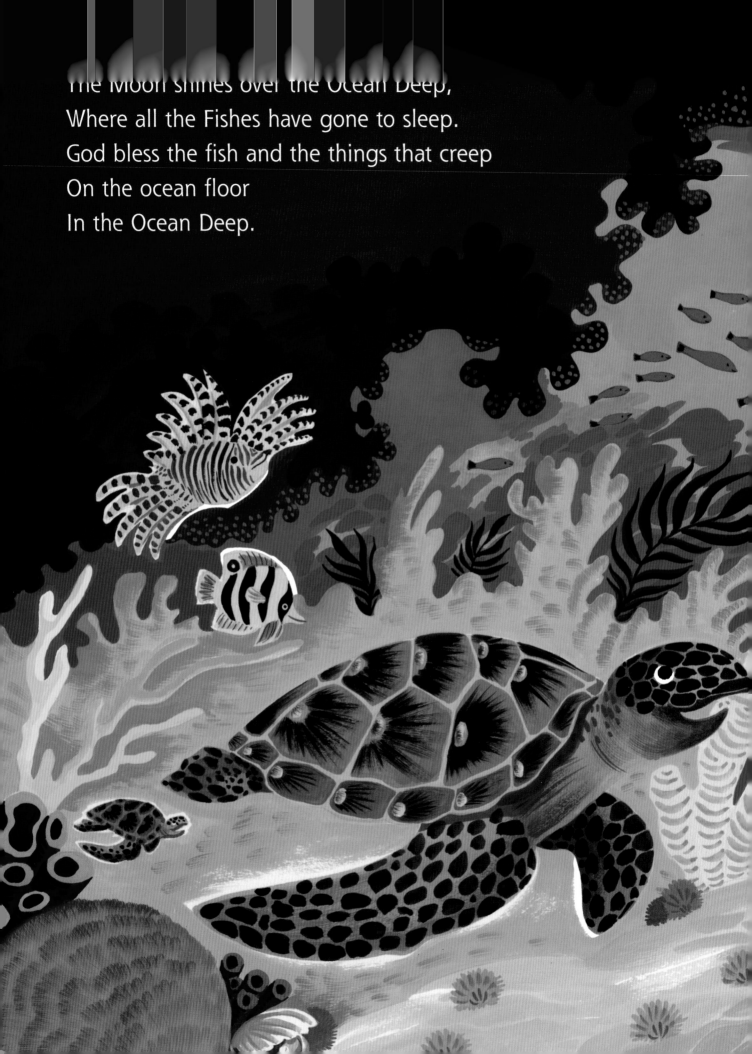

The Moon shines over the Ocean Deep,
Where all the Fishes have gone to sleep.
God bless the fish and the things that creep
On the ocean floor
In the Ocean Deep.

So God bless the Moon
And God bless me,
And God bless the creatures
In the Big Blue Sea.

I see the Moon and the Moon sees me,
And all the children in every country—
In Australia, Norway, and Italy,
Africa, Japan, and Germany.

I see the Moon
And the Moon sees me.
God bless the Moon
And God bless me.